Sir Gadabout
and the
Camelot Calamity

Martyn Beardsley

Sir Gadabout
and the
Camelot Calamity

Illustrated by Tony Ross

Orion
Children's Books

First published in Great Britain in 2008
by Orion Children's Books
a division of the Orion Publishing Group Ltd
Orion House
5 Upper St Martin's Lane
London WC2H 9EA
An Hachette Livre UK Company

1 3 5 7 9 10 8 6 4 2

Text copyright © Martyn Beardsley 2008
Illustrations copyright © Tony Ross 2008

A catalogue record for this book
is available from the British Library

The Orion Publishing Group's policy is to use papers that
are natural, renewable and recyclable products and made
from wood grown in sustainable forests. The logging and
manufacturing processes are expected to conform to the
environmental regulations of the country of origin.

Printed in Great Britain by Clays Ltd, St Ives plc

ISBN 978 1 84255 616 0

www.orionbooks.co.uk

Contents

1 Problem Pets   1

2 Twaddle and Twaddle   13

3 The Crystal of Correction   27

4 Royal Twaddle   39

5 Trapped!   51

6 Up and Away!   65

7 Tanks for the Help   77

Problem Pets

A long, long time ago – well before fridge magnets were invented and everyone had to stare at boring white fridge doors all day long – there was a famous castle called Camelot.

Camelot was a mighty fortress hidden in a dim and misty corner of the land – which unfortunately made it quite tricky for the postman to find. One of the Knights of the Round Table sent a postcard from his holidays in Skegness in 1984 and it still hasn't arrived to this day.

Within Camelot lived King Arthur. He was famed for his wisdom and bravery – and also his huge collection of Flags of the World stickers, which he ordered from *Majesty Monthly* magazine and stuck in a big album (free with Issue One). It was his ambition to become the first monarch to fill the album up, but he was still waiting for Serbia and Montenegro which he had ordered *ages* ago. He was beginning to wonder whether the postman had delivered it to Arthur King again, who lived in nearby Chipping Sodnorton. Arthur King had once received Equatorial Guinea by mistake and had been so reluctant to give it up that a deputation of knights had to be sent to get it off him.

Alongside King Arthur at Camelot was Queen Guinevere. Guinevere was not only beautiful and just as wise as King Arthur, but she was also very handy with her hammer and nails. Not a lot of people realise that Camelot's famous Round Table, which all the brave knights sat at, was originally square. Sir Andrew the Ample kept catching his legs on the corners and coming out in a nasty bruise, so in the end Guinevere got her tools out, rounded the corners off, and while she was at it she evened up the wobbly legs and gave it a smart coat of varnish.

One bright summer's morning, King Arthur was on his way to the Post Office to enquire after his Serbia and Montenegro flag when Sir Lancelot happened to pass by with a dog on a lead.

"Morning, Sir Lancelot. I didn't know you had a dog," said King Arthur.

"Oh, I've only just got him, your majesty. He's very clever. Look at this—"

Sir Lancelot took off one of his boots and threw it as far as he could, crying, *"Fetch, Rover!"* The dog scampered off, picked the boot up in its mouth and returned it to the knight.

"Well, I think lots of dogs can do that, Sir Lancelot," said the king. "Maybe you could teach it to . . . "

He stopped what he was saying and began to stare open-mouthed. Not only had the dog brought the boot back, but he had put it back on Sir Lancelot's foot, and, by using a clever combination of his paws, teeth and tongue, was tying the lace. And he did a double knot! (The laces were a bit too long and Sir Lancelot kept tripping over them.)

"That's amazing!" said King Arthur.

"That's not all," said Sir Lancelot proudly. He gave a few more commands, and Rover proceeded to write the answers to some very complicated sums by scratching with his paws on the dusty ground (including long division, which had always baffled King Arthur). He (Rover, not King Arthur) then

showed his athletic prowess by demonstrating two cartwheels, three back-flips, and a somersault. He finished on a Double-Eisenhower with pike, which even Olympic gymnasts have problems with. Rover finally landed on his head and managed to walk twelve metres using only his ears.

"And I haven't been training him for long," said Sir Lancelot proudly. "I only got him a week ago from Pittance's Pet Shop in Camelot village."

"I never knew he sold such amazing pets," said the king.

"It's under new ownership. Everything's changed there now!"

"It's a shame, because I liked old Simon Pittance who used to run it."

"Ah, but Mr and Mrs Twaddle who own it now have some *much* more exciting ideas!" said Sir Lancelot.

King Arthur carried on, and just before he reached the Post Office he came across Sir Gavin the Greasy. Sir Gavin seemed to be talking to someone, so the king didn't want to disturb him. But on closer inspection, it didn't look like there was anyone actually with Sir Gavin. When the king got closer still, however, he could see a parrot sitting on a fence.

"I'm very pleased with you, Polly," Sir Gavin the Greasy was saying. "You have learned to talk so quickly!"

"Being of South American descent, I found your rather thick West Country accent quite hard to understand at first," replied Polly. "But I must admit I am quite pleased with my progress thus far."

King Arthur could hardly believe his ears. "That's the cleverest parrot I've ever seen or heard!" he exclaimed.

"Actually, the ability to talk is not always a sign of cleverness," Polly pointed out. "Many birds can mimic the human voice and other sounds without actually understanding what they are saying. In my case, however, you are right – I am extremely brainy."

"Er . . . oh, I'm sure you are," said the king.

"Funnily enough, Your Majesty," said Sir

Gavin, "Polly was saying only the other day that she would quite like to have a debate with you – about whether countries should be run by a monarchy or an elected parliament."

King Arthur wasn't quite sure what all that meant, but he somehow didn't like the sound of it. "I'd love to, but I must get along to the Post Office. Where did you get her from, anyway?"

"*She's* got a name, you know!" said the parrot.

"Sorry – where did you get Polly from?"

"Simon Pittance's pet shop in Camelot village. It's great since Mr and Mrs Twaddle took over!"

"So I've heard. I quite liked old Mr Pittance, but never mind."

Just as the king was leaving, Sir Gavin the Greasy proudly called after him, "She can also say *Who's a pretty Polly?*, Your Majesty. I taught her that yesterday!"

King Arthur thought he heard the parrot let out a long sigh.

Once he got back to Camelot (sadly, still without his flag sticker) King Arthur was walking past the room where the Crown Jewels were kept when he saw Queen Guinevere standing at the open door.

"Hello, my dear," he said. "Are you inspecting the Royal Valuables?"

"I'm not – it's Sir Bumptious and his pet."

"Not another one . . ."

"He's got a magpie and it's sorting everything out in here. It *was* rather a mess – and it's amazing what the bird can do."

"Well, my dear, it's well known that magpies are attracted to shiny things and like to pick them up and move them around."

"Yes, my love, but this one is arranging them into categories according to value, rarity and hallmark. He's just sorted the rubies from the emeralds."

King Arthur poked his head around the door. The magpie was standing on top of a heap of glittering gold crowns, diamond brooches, tiaras and other impressive items. He was picking them up with his beak and throwing them into different piles all around him.

"That's worth a bob or two," he said, tossing a silver bracelet with inlaid diamonds. "That's a load of rubbish," he continued, throwing a golden goblet with sapphires round the rim onto a different pile.

"Oh, and he can talk," added Queen Guinevere.

"I noticed. But that goblet is worth millions!" cried the king. "It was given to us

by Sir Frederick the Futile as an anniversary present."

"Worthless tat, gov'n'r," insisted the magpie. "Just a bit o' polished brass and coloured glass. I could get you something better by hooking a duck at a fair."

"Isn't he wonderful?" said Sir Bumptious. "I got him—"

"Let me guess – from Pittance's Pet Shop?" said the king wearily.

"How did you know?"

"It seems like everyone at Camelot's got a pet from there these days."

"Except us!" said Guinevere. "We've always wanted a nice little kitten – I'm told they've got some really cute ones. Shall we?"

"Well . . ."

"Please?!"

"Well . . ."

"Pretty please?!"

"Oh, all right then!"

King Arthur was very impressed by the pets that seemed to be coming from Pittance's Pet Shop, and he liked the idea of

a cute kitten as much as Guinevere. It was just that he was sad about going back to the pet shop now that old Mr Pittance had gone. And anyway, there was something that didn't seem quite right about the things these wonderful animals that all the knights were getting could do . . .

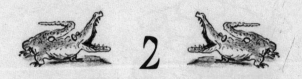

2

Twaddle and Twaddle

Before buying a cute kitten from Pittance's Pet Shop, King Arthur decided to send a knight to investigate the place and see what exactly was going on there. He sent one of the Royal Messengers round Camelot to see who was available, and was told that there was only one knight free. The rest were out fighting dragons, saving damsels in distress, or doing the weekly shopping. When he heard who this knight was, King Arthur sent the messenger out again. Was there *anyone* else who could go – perhaps a guard, or a toilet attendant, or a tea lady?

But no, everyone was busy except one

knight. The reason the king was a little reluctant was that this particular knight every now and then got into a little bit of a pickle. Only sometimes, though. Mostly, he got into a Very Big Pickle. King Arthur was particularly nervous because this particular knight had recently been sent to buy a bag of cheese and onion crisps from the Camelot KwikMart for Guinevere. By the time he had returned, the KwikMart and three other shops had been demolished by a

runaway bulldozer, which this particular knight had accidentally set into motion. The knight had then been chased by an angry mob, and his horse had trampled through the Best Kept Garden in Camelot competition winner just as the prize was being awarded, upon which a second angry mob joined in the chase. And after all that he came back to Camelot with a packet of *salt and vinegar* crisps, which Guinevere hated.

He was known by all and sundry as the

Worst Knight in the World, and his name was Sir Gadabout. The only person who refused to believe that Sir Gadabout was the Worst Knight in the World was his faithful squire Herbert. Herbert was a short but stocky youth who accompanied Sir Gadabout on all his adventures – and woe betide anyone who said bad things about his master when he was around!

When the Royal messenger arrived to tell King Arthur that Sir Gadabout was here to see him, the poor man was pale and trembling.

"What's the matter?" asked the king. "Are you feeling ill?"

"N–no, Your Majesty. It's . . . it's . . . He's brought his *pet* with him."

"You mean he's already been to Pittance's Pet Shop?"

"No, Your Majesty. Someone else got it, but Sir Gadabout agreed to look after it when it got . . . a bit too big for him."

"Well, what sort of pet is it?"

"He says it's a lizard, Your Majesty."

When Sir Gadabout was shown in, almost everyone else left – in a big hurry, screaming and shrieking. King Arthur himself hid behind his throne.

"Has the fire alarm gone off again, Your Majesty?" asked Sir Gadabout.

"W–what's *that*?"

"It's Lizzy, Your Majesty! She's a lizard. *Lizzy-lizard* – do you get it, Your Majesty?"

"Sir Gadabout . . . " squeaked King Arthur

from behind his throne. "Lizzy is a CROCODILE!"

"Oh, no, Your Majesty. Crocodiles are big, dangerous, nasty beasts."

"But that *is* big – and it looks nasty and dangerous to me!" quailed the king.

"Lizzy is quite harmless and cuddly," Sir Gadabout assured the king, patting the beast on the head. Lizzy followed Sir Gadabout's hand with two beady eyes, and a little dribble emerged from the corner of her mouth. "She was supposed to be a Madagascan Miniature lizard, but it seems the pet shop made a small mistake and she's turned out to be a Latvian Large. Mr and Mrs Twaddle have apparently promised she's definitely not, on the whole, a crocodile, Your Majesty."

"Well, Sir Gadabout, if you wouldn't mind taking your *Latvian Large* back to the shop just to double check, I'd be very grateful. And while you're there, try to find out exactly what's going on at Pittance's Pet Shop. Something doesn't seem quite right to me."

"Right away, Your Majesty. But wouldn't you like to look after little Lizzy while I go and talk to them?"

"NOOOOO!" bellowed the king in a strange voice almost like someone about to fall off a cliff. "I mean – no, thank you, Sir Gadabout. That will be all!"

Sir Gadabout and his squire Herbert duly set off for the pet shop, not too far away in the little village near the castle. After they had left Camelot, it was discovered that one of the Royal Messengers had gone missing. He was never found – but someone said they saw Lizzy licking her lips on the way out . . .

Sir Gadabout and Herbert noticed, as they approached the shop, that its sign had been altered. *Pittance's Pet Shop* had a line drawn through it, and *TWADDLE AND TWADDLE'S PERFECT PETS* had been clumsily daubed underneath in green paint, with lots of blotches and runs.

Just before they could go in, the door flew open and a woman emerged dragging a

small, petrified little man by the collar. *"And don't come back!"* she screeched.

"But I only wanted a budgie!" he complained.

"We only serve Knights of the Round Table, not riff-raff like you," the woman said, giving him a final kick to the bottom before turning and going back into the shop.

As he staggered towards Sir Gadabout and Herbert, little Lizzy suddenly bared her teeth and lunged at the man like a . . . well, like a crocodile. Luckily, Herbert managed to pull the man out of the way just in time. When the poor chap saw what had nearly had him for lunch, his hair stood on end. (I know people some-times say that – but this time it *really did*!) He shrieked so loudly that the window of the nearby Camelot KwikMart (which had just been replaced)  shattered, and he ran for his life. They say he didn't stop running till he reached Baffin Bay, where he was adopted by a family of Eskimo and lived to the ripe old age of ninety-nine.

"I think Lizzy wanted to lick his hand – she's so sweet!" said Sir Gadabout. (This was before the man reached Baffin Bay, of course. He had probably got no further than Woolacombe by then.)

"Possibly, sire . . . " replied Herbert. And they went into the shop.

"Aargh! GET OUT!" cried the woman

who had kicked the little man out (who was somewhere near Weston-Super-Mare by now).

"But madam, I am a Knight of the Round Table," announced Sir Gadabout. "I distinctly heard you telling that gentleman that we could come to your shop."

"But you can't bring that savage animal in here," squawked the woman. "It'll have someone's arm off!" The woman had straggly black hair and a hooked nose with a wart on the end. She wore a shabby green uniform which looked like it had been home-made (and not very well at that). And there was a badge pinned to her uniform which said: *Twaddle and Twaddle: Pets by Royal Appointment*.

"But it came from this pet shop!" Herbert protested.

The woman scowled and roared, *"MR TWADDLE!"*

A man emerged from a back room. "Not now – I'm just putting a spell on this guinea p—" He stopped suddenly when he saw Sir

Gadabout and Herbert. "I mean — I'm just teaching this guinea pig how to spell . . ." Mr Twaddle looked remarkably like Mrs Twaddle — but for a strangely gruff voice and a beard which seemed to have sticky-tape showing at the edges.

"A spelling guinea pig!" cried Sir Gadabout. "I could do with one of those."

"I'm not sure he really said that . . ." whispered Herbert.

"I wonder if they're cheaper than dictionaries?" Sir Gadabout continued, checking how much money he had with him.

"In fact," whispered Herbert, "I'm not even sure *he's* really a *he*! And their voices seem familiar . . ."

"What do you want?" said Mr Twaddle in his strange husky voice. "We don't give refunds."

Just then, what looked like a gorilla came bursting out of the back room, crying, *"Help! Save me!"*

The two Twaddles quickly bundled the gorilla back into the other room.

"What an exciting pet shop!" said Sir Gadabout. "A spelling guinea pig – and a gorilla with a voice like Simon Pittance, the old pet shop man!"

"Well, I don't like it," Herbert replied. "Let's go – we'd better report all this back to King Arthur."

Once they had gone, Albert Spritely the old pet shop assistant couldn't be found anywhere. It's possible that the fright of seeing little Lizzy made him run away – but as Sir Gadabout and Herbert were leaving, Lizzy was licking her lips and had what looked like a bit of green uniform stuck between her teeth . . .

3

The Crystal of Correction

Things had got worse at Camelot by the time Sir Gadabout and Herbert arrived back. Sir Lancelot's dog had continued to grow, and now looked suspiciously like a wolf. It was sitting growling outside his door and not letting him out. Several other knights had bought pets which were keeping them prisoner. Sir Nastismel had got a cute little kitten (making Guinevere very jealous). But it had grown and grown, so was now very hard to tell apart from a tiger, and was guarding Sir Nastismel's door, letting out the occasional terrifying roar. On top of it all, Sir Bumptious's parrot contacted someone he knew at the local paper and made a convincing case for getting rid of the royal family.

When King Arthur picked up the *Camelot Courier* and saw the headline: "IS THIS THE END FOR THE ROYALS? EXCLUSIVE INSIDE STORY – ROYAL PARROT TELLS ALL!" he made an instant, kingly decision: Something Must Be Done. The trouble was, he couldn't think what – so he had a word with Guinevere.

On being told by Sir Gadabout about the spelling guinea pig – or the guinea pig under a spell – and the gorilla that sounded like Simon Pittance, Guinevere decided that there was only one person who could help him to sort it out. Merlin the wizard!

Sir Gadabout and Herbert left the castle (thankfully leaving little Lizzy securely locked in Sir Gadabout's room) and made their way through the murky and mysterious Willow Wood until they came to the great magician's cottage. They opened the rickety garden gate as quietly and carefully as they could – on past visits, very strange things had happened at about this time. But all seemed very quiet. They walked down the winding garden path, looking for shocks or surprises, but still nothing happened.

"The garden seems a bit more overgrown than last time," whispered Sir Gadabout.

"Yes," Herbert agreed. "I don't remember that big bush being there either."

They crept past the big bush, but still nothing untoward happened. At the front door was a cord which looked like it was for a doorbell, and a little sign next to it saying, "PULL HARD". So Sir Gadabout pulled hard. There was no ringing of a bell – but they heard a noise behind them and wheeled round.

What they had thought was a bush was really camouflage, and in pulling the cord they had whipped it away to reveal – a TANK! It was actually a home-made one, created from old wooden boxes and tins, with a long barrel made from a drainpipe. Dr McPherson, Merlin's guard turtle sat in the turret wearing a crazy grin, and there was a pile of ammunition on the side of the tank next to him. The "ammunition" was actually melons – but they were pretty big and fearsome looking ones.

"FIRE!" cried Dr McPherson. He pressed

a button somewhere inside his tank. There was a rumble. There was a shudder. BOOM!

Sir Gadabout and Herbert ducked, and just at that moment the cottage door was opened by Sidney Smith, Merlin's sarcastic cat. "What's all this . . . WAAAAAH!" The melon hit him right in the chops and splattered all over the place. But Dr McPherson had made the gun in his tank a bit too powerful. As the melon shot forwards, the tank shot backwards at an even greater rate. It smashed through the garden fence and just kept going. It is believed to have come to a halt in the middle of the Battle of Hastings, where it played a vital role in holding off the formidable Norman attacks – until Dr McPherson unfortunately ran out of melons.

"I'll give that barmy turtle the sack!" spluttered Sidney Smith, wiping the gunge from his whiskers.

"We have come to see Merlin on a very important matter," Sir Gadabout announced grandly.

"Well, Merlin's busy, so push off," said the cat, who was now in an even worse mood than usual.

He tried to slam the door on them, but Herbert was too quick and managed to put his foot in the doorway to stop it being closed.

"What is the meaning of this?" came a deep and commanding voice. It was Merlin, the world's greatest wizard, in his long flowing cloak with silver moons and stars on it.

"It's these bungling baboons from Camelot," said Sidney Smith. "It'll take *weeks* to lick all of this melon out of my fur!"

"Let them in, if you please," ordered Merlin. He knew that King Arthur didn't send his knights unless he was in desperate need of help. And when he sent Sir Gadabout, Merlin knew he was very desperate.

The story of Simon Pittance's pet shop and the Twaddles was explained to him, and Merlin stroked his long grey beard thoughtfully. Several spiders and a couple of mice fled from it and ran down his cloak.

"Hmmm . . . This sounds like powerful magic indeed. What you need is the *Crystal of Correction*!" He went over to a big table, moved some great dusty spell books and bottles of magic potion, and picked up a crystal ball. He wiped the dust away on his baggy sleeve, and the ball shone in the candlelight which lit the room. Although it was as clear as glass, depending on how you held it, it seemed to flash with all the colours of the rainbow (except the ones you can't see, of course. It might have flashed with those too but we just can't say for sure).

Merlin showed them how the Crystal of Correction worked. With a wave of his wand and a few magic words, he turned Herbert into a Staffordshire Bull terrier.

"That mutt's much better looking than Herbert!" sniggered Sidney Smith.

The dog – I mean, Herbert – barked angrily.

"And he makes more sense too!" the cat added.

"And now, to put things right, we use the Crystal of Correction . . . " Merlin held the ball aloft and uttered the magic words: "*Reverso – Change it back!*"

A crackly flash of blueish-white light, like miniature lightning, snaked out of the crystal ball and struck the dog between the eyes. He was instantly turned back into Herbert.

"I'm my old self again!" said the squire in amazement. "Can we go walkies now?"

Sidney Smith chuckled and threw a stick. "Fetch, Rover!"

"Yes, well," muttered Merlin as Herbert ran after it with his tongue hanging out. "It does take a little time for *all* the effects to wear off . . . "

Sir Gadabout was delighted. "We'll soon have Camelot back to normal!"

"You must be careful," said Merlin, handing him the crystal.

"With this wonderful thing what could go wrong?"

"When *you're* involved, mate," said Sidney Smith, "*anything* can go wrong."

Merlin now turned poor Herbert into a cat with a wave of his wand so that Sir Gadabout could practise on him.

"Hey – there's no room for any more cats in *this* house!" Sidney Smith complained.

"Now," said Merlin, "shout *Reverso – Change it back* and point the beam at him."

"Easy-peasy!" replied Sir Gadabout. He raised the crystal ball into the air. "Er . . . *Reverse it Back!*"

The flash of lightning missed Herbert and hit Sidney Smith, who turned into a large rat which squeaked indignantly. On hearing the squeaks, Herbert, still a cat, pounced and just

missed. A frantic chase ensued which just about wrecked Merlin's cottage. The great wizard quickly grabbed the Crystal of Correction and put things to rights.

"Now you can see why it's necessary to be very careful with the Crystal of Correction!" Merlin warned Sir Gadabout. "I suggest you go and visit these Twaddle people first and see what they are *really* up to. You can sort Camelot out later."

"Very wise advice," agreed Sir Gadabout.

"Yes," said Herbert. "But I'm hungry. Can we go and buy a nice juicy bone on the way? I mean – a nice piece of fish and a saucer of milk! *No!* I mean . . . "

Sidney Smith chuckled loudly.

"And," interrupted Merlin, "I'm going to send Sidney Smith with you to make sure I get my crystal ball back in one piece."

The cat clapped a paw to his head. *"Awwwww!"*

Royal Twaddle

On the way to see Mr and Mrs Twaddle, Sir Gadabout, Herbert and Sidney Smith came across a commotion in the road. A man with a horse was involved in a furious argument with another man standing by an overturned cart. The cart had been carrying a load of fruit and vegetables for the Camelot market, and all the goods were now scattered on the ground.

"It's not my fault," shouted the man with the horse. He was a very big man with a broken nose like a boxer, and he had large hands with lots of rings on his fingers with gold coins in them. "You oughta look where you're going, you scrimpled load of old scragglepoop!" (That's how people used to swear in those days.)

"Don't you call *me* a scrimpled load of old scragglepoop, you mangly great guzzock!" said the other man, who was even bigger and uglier. "Your blathersome chuggwallop of a horse scared mine – and now look what's happened!"

The men clenched their fists and began to walk towards one another.

Sir Gadabout approached them. "This is just the sort of situation where a Knight of the Round Table is meant to restore peace."

"By the looks of them, it'll be you that's 'Resting in Peace'," chortled Sidney Smith.

"Now, now, my good gentlemen, let's not raise our voices," said Sir Gadabout.

The two men stopped arguing and turned towards him.

"And who are you to tell me not to raise my voice, you sproggle-nosed pile of tin-cans," said the first man, raising his voice even louder.

"Yes – what's it got to do with you,

40

shmuzzle-face?" yelled the other man.

"I am a Knight of the Round Table, and I can sort this mess out in a jiffy with my Crystal of Connection so that everything's just as it was before!"

"*Correction*, sire," Herbert pointed out.

Sir Gadabout looked at him for a moment. "Well?"

"'Well' what?"

"I thought you said you were going to correct me . . . "

"But I just have . . . "

"Never mind whether it's correction or connection," said the two men. "You can really sort all this mess out?"

"I don't think it will work quite how you think . . . " Sidney Smith warned Sir Gadabout.

"Nonsense," said Sir Gadabout. "I've got the hang of this thing now." He raised the crystal ball and aimed it at the fruit and vegetables on the ground.

"Well, remember the words are: *Reverso – Change it Back*, sire," said Herbert worriedly.

"Fear not," Sir Gadabout assured him. *"Reverse – oh please change back!"*

The word itself was close enough. The problem was that Sidney Smith had been right – the crystal put things back to the way they had been before they had been changed – by a spell, for example. As the fruit and vegetables hadn't been *changed* into anything but were just lying on the floor, the spell changed them back to what they had once been – *seeds*!

When the bigger man saw his lovely fresh produce suddenly become a handful of tiny seeds scattered in the dust, he began to growl in a most alarming manner and stomp towards Sir Gadabout. And the other man might have been his enemy, but he wasn't going to miss out on a good fight and the chance to pick on someone smaller, so he joined the first one.

"A-a-at least th-th-they won't be so heavy to pick up now, peaceful gentlemen . . . " stuttered Sir Gadabout. He was shaking so much that his armour began to sound like

an out of tune wind chime on a stormy day.

"You're the one who will need picking up, you blathering numbskull," smirked Sidney Smith.

"And that cat's having a laugh at us — let's get him too!" the angry men muttered.

"*Ooer!*" miaowed Sidney Smith, his smile quickly disappearing as he scarpered up the nearest tree.

Herbert quickly jumped up with Sir Gadabout on his horse, and at the knight's command it ran as fast as it could away from the pursuers. Which wasn't very fast at all. In fact, when they were overtaken by a caterpillar on its way back from eating some cabbages in a nearby garden, they decided it might be better to jump off and run.

Luckily for them, the two men stopped when they got into an argument about whether they should also fight the horse. One said it was laughing at them, the other said it was just whinnying, and horses always looked like that when they whinnied. It was a difficult point to settle, but the very big man finally won the argument by biffing the fairly big one on the nose. By then, fortunately, they'd forgotten about chasing Sir Gadabout and Herbert, and once Sidney Smith had caught up they resumed their journey to the pet shop.

When they got there, it looked very different.

The door was locked and bolted, and the windows were boarded up. A sign had been stuck on the door. There was lots of spidery green writing scrawled on it, which said:

Mr and Mrs Twaddle would like to thank all customers for their support (except the riff-raff), but would like to proudly announce that they are packing in this pet shop lark as they have recently

been crowned King and Queen. Quite right too —
that Camelot gang are frauds and impostors!
King Detritus Twaddle promises to be much fairer
and wiser than the liar and cheat Arthur. And
although Queen Timidity Twaddle isn't that good
at woodwork yet, she promises to go on a course
and become better at it than Girly Guinevere,
who couldn't knock a nail in a barn door from ten
paces. Okay, we know that would be hard for
anyone — unless they had very long arms. But you
know what we mean — unless you are a raving
fool like the old king and queen and the rest of
that lot at the castle. And if you say we're not the
real king and queen, we'll come and sort you out.
Love and best wishes, King and Queen Twaddle.

"Well, well," said Sir Gadabout. "I always
thought Arthur and Guinevere were the real
king and queen — shows you how wrong
you can be!"

"You dundering barmpot!" cried Sidney
Smith.

"And they did sound familiar — almost like
. . . Morag and Demelza!" said Herbert.

"Morag and Demelza!" exclaimed Sir Gadabout and Sidney Smith at the same time.

Morag and Demelza were two cunning and meddlesome witches whom they had come up against more than once in the past.

"We must hurry back to Camelot!" said Herbert. "Who knows what they've got up to with all those strange animals on the loose."

The three of them had turned and started to hurry away, when Sidney Smith cried, "Wait – what's that noise?"

"It's my stomach," said Sir Gadabout sheepishly. "I didn't have any breakfast."

"No, you noggin, not that noise. It sounded like banging."

"Now I can hear it too!" agreed Herbert.

"Well, it could be my boots," said Sir Gadabout. "You see, the heel's coming off one of them, and every time I take a step—"

They ignored him and went back to the pet shop, where the *real* noise seemed to be coming from. There was definitely someone banging inside – and the sound of muffled cries for help.

"Someone needs help. We'll have to force our way in!" said Herbert.

"Ah!" said Sir Gadabout. "This is where a Knight of the Round Table comes into his own!" He picked up his long lance, climbed onto his horse, and got ready to charge the door.

All this took quite some time, and meanwhile Herbert had simply given the door a powerful push with his shoulder and kick with his foot, and bashed his way in. He and Sidney Smith were shocked to find a gorilla lying on the floor, all tied up with rope. But before they could run away again, it said, "*I'm not a gorilla!* I'm Peter Pittance – two horrible witches left me like this!"

"Don't worry, Mr Pittance," said Herbert. "We'll rescue—"

At that moment, Sir Gadabout, who had finally managed to get his slowcoach horse to charge, flew past crying, "*WHO OPENED THE DOOOOOOR??!!!*" His lance just missed Herbert's nose, went right through Sidney Smith's whiskers, and stuck in the rope tied round Peter Pittance. With the gorilla on the end of his lance, Sir Gadabout crashed straight through the shop and burst out through the back door. The horse, who hadn't had a good old charge in ages, was by now quite enjoying himself and not about to stop. Fortunately, they were heading straight in the direction of Camelot!

5

Trapped!

When Sir Gadabout arrived at Camelot castle with a gorilla on the end of his lance, the only person he found around was King Arthur himself – but he was up a flagpole with a pack of hyenas circling and snapping at his heels. Now, it's a little known fact that hyenas are terrified of gorillas. The yapping creatures vanished in a trice when Sir Gadabout arrived, and King Arthur was able to slide down the pole.

"Thank goodness!" he gasped. "Camelot is in turmoil! There are dangerous beasts everywhere. They are all under the power of those horrible pet shop people – and *they* are sitting on my and Guinevere's thrones giving out orders and changing laws left, right and centre!"

"Don't worry, Your Majesty," said Sir Gadabout calmly. "We believe that Mr and Mrs Twaddle are none other than the witches Morag and Demelza. But I've managed to rescue Simon Pittance, the real pet shop owner, from the clutches of . . . er . . . Herbert and Sidney Smith."

"Eh?"

"It's a long story, Your Majesty. But I also have *this*!" and he proudly revealed the Crystal of Correction. "I can put everything back to just the way it was with Merlin's marvellous device – starting with poor Mr Pittance."

Sir Gadabout aimed the crystal at Simon.

"Now . . . what were those words?"

"But I'm not a gorilla," said the pet shop man.

"I know you're not, my good man. Was it *Reverse Come Back*?"

"You don't understand!" insisted Simon. "You mustn't try the spell!"

"Now, now," said Sir Gadabout. "Don't be a baby. *The verse is back!*"

And in an instant, Simon Pittance was a baby! He had been trying to tell Sir Gadabout that he hadn't been changed into a gorilla by a spell, but simply zipped up in a gorilla suit. So the spell changed him back into what he used to be – a tiny infant.

"Oops!" said Sir Gadabout.

"Whaaaah! Whaaaah!" whimpered Simon Pittance, who had a touch of wind.

"What's wrong with him?" asked the king.

"Never fear, Your Majesty. My sister had one of those things. They always either need feeding or their nappy changing when they make that noise."

"I don't mean what's wrong with him!" said the exasperated king. "I mean . . . what's *wrong* with him! What have you done?"

Sir Gadabout examined the crystal and gave it a shake. "It seems to be this thing. Maybe the batteries are running low or something."

Just then, Herbert and Sidney Smith came

huffing and puffing along. Seeing a bawling baby nestling in the black fur of a gorilla suit, Herbert scratched his head.

"*Now* what's happened, sire?"

Sidney Smith groaned.

"I don't even want to know . . ."

Once everything had been explained, King Arthur said, "We really ought to go and sort Morag and Demelza out − but I'm not sure we'll even get that far with all these savage animals around."

"We need to go and get Merlin," said Sidney Smith.

The king shook his head. "There's a pack of baboons on guard there. You should see the size of their teeth! Has anyone got a good idea?"

"Your Majesty," declared Sir Gadabout, "I shall mount my horse, take my sharpest lance, and charge the baboons!"

"Yeah," muttered Sidney Smith. "Like he said − has anyone got a *good* idea?"

"*The gorilla suit!*" cried Herbert out of the blue.

"The gorilla suit can't come up with a good idea," said Sir Gadabout. "It's only a costume. We all thought it was real but—"

"No," insisted Herbert. "A mighty gorilla would frighten most animals away. If I put it on at least we might stand a chance."

"Ah, yes. That's what I thought you meant . . . " said Sir Gadabout.

"Excellent thinking!" King Arthur said. "It certainly sent those hyenas running."

So, Herbert put the costume on and away they went.

There were two problems.

Firstly, some, but by no means all animals are afraid of gorillas. Elephants, for example. And lions. Oh, and tigers, wolves . . . In fact there are quite a lot of animals which aren't afraid of gorillas! And secondly, Herbert was much too short to fill the costume. For every step he took inside the suit, the gorilla was only taking one step. Herbert's head didn't reach the top, so the gorilla's head was flopping all over the place as if he was drunk. To make matters worse, Herbert kept stumbling and tripping, and rolling around inside the fur costume. Not many animals are thought to be afraid of a drunken gorilla . . .

As they made their way through Camelot's maze of corridors, they first came upon a writhing mass of slithery snakes – all with a deadly poison in their bite – keeping many of the knights trapped inside their rooms. Snakes aren't particularly afraid of gorillas – but when they saw a big ball of fur rolling and tumbling towards them, uttering strange cries, they thought it must be some kind of strange beast they'd never encountered before. They scarpered up the nearest drainpipe and were never seen again. (Until the plumber was called some weeks later to see what was causing a blockage. Gave him quite a fright, as you can imagine.)

Sir Gadabout and Co. pressed on towards the armoury. All the castle's weapons were kept there, and a swarm of hairy, poisonous tarantulas and other huge, scary spiders was keeping guard to prevent any knights getting

to them. But when they saw the great hairy ball with flailing arms and legs coming their way, they thought it must be the biggest spider in the world. They all scuttled under the nearest door to hide in a chest of drawers, and were never seen again. (Until Sir Lumbago returned to his room to look for a clean pair of socks. They say the poor chap ran so fast his shoes caught fire.)

"I think I must make a pretty realistic gorilla!" came a muffled but proud voice from inside the costume as he picked himself up once more.

"*Pretty*' isn't a word I would have used myself," Sidney Smith muttered.

Now, they were coming to the most dangerous area – the Great Hall – where Morag and Demelza were sitting on the thrones of Arthur and Guinevere, above which was stuck a sign scribbled in green ink: UNDER NEW MANAGEMENT. But there were no wild animals here. The two witches were so sure that their magic was a match for anyone else's that they

hadn't bothered with any protection of that kind.

"I, King Detritus Twaddle, do declare and command," the impostor king was announcing to a poor quivering scribe, "that from this day forth and hence, and hereafter, and all that, that all the lord mayors in the land shall be kicked out and replaced by witches!"

"NO!" cried King Arthur.

"And I, Queen Timidity Twaddle, do announce and decree and rule and command and—"

"Yes, yes, don't overdo all this royal talk,"

moaned Morag, who was pretending to be the king.

"I'm the queen and I'll do what I jolly well like! I hereby declare and proclaim and order and instruct and . . . well, that's enough anyway. I command, and all the rest heretofore, that all the daft Knights of the Round Table shall be kicked out and ejected and sent packing and—"

"Get on with it for goodness' sake!" said Morag.

"—and expelled – and made to work as pig stye cleaners and live with the pigs . . ."

"NO!" yelled Arthur again.

"But I quite like pigs . . ." Sir Gadabout said.

"Ah!" said Morag, noticing the new arrivals. "Here's the blundering buffoon himself!"

"How *dare* you talk to His Majesty like that!" exclaimed Sir Gadabout.

"I meant you!" said Morag.

"Oh . . ."

"Just you wait till I get my hands on you,"

roared Herbert on hearing his master insulted. It looked like a fight was going on inside the gorilla suit as Herbert struggled to find his way out.

"He's not a gorilla, he's a cheeky little monkey!" Demelza commented. "So let's turn him into one!"

"Quick, stop them with the crystal!" King Arthur urged Sir Gadabout. He didn't know exactly what it would turn the witches into, but at least it would be better than nothing.

"I don't like the sound of this . . . " said Sidney Smith.

Sir Gadabout plucked the Crystal of Correction from his pocket and pointed it at Morag who was waving her arms about and beginning to chant a spell.

"*Reduce it and change it back!*" he cried. Unfortunately, Sir Gadabout's hands were shaking so much that he missed Morag and hit the throne with the beam of blue-white lightning. It immediately turned into the pile of wood and nails it used to be (only much smaller), and Morag fell in a heap on the floor.

"Oh well, better luck this time . . . " He turned the crystal on Demelza, who was also

trying to cast a spell. The blue beam shot past the witch and hit Polly the parrot, who had left Sir Gavin the Greasy and was now on a perch above Demelza. Polly turned into an egg – and landed with a splat on Demelza's head.

Seeing that the two witches were thrown into confusion for the moment, King Arthur cried, "CHARGE!" and ran at them. All the others charged too. Except Herbert, who sort of rolled and tumbled. And Sir Gadabout, who had dropped the crystal and was scrabbling about under the Round Table for it.

The battle was far from over.

A door at the far end of the Great Hall burst open, and through it came a pride of the biggest and most ferocious lions the world has ever known. With roars and snarls, they began to prowl menacingly towards the king and his followers.

"This way!" commanded the king, turning to run back through the door they had come in through.

But then through this door leapt an ambush of tigers, growling threateningly and flashing their razor-sharp claws towards the king and the rest of them.

There was no way out.

6

Up and Away!

King Arthur and his group huddled together in fear, waiting to see what was going to happen next – all except Sir Gadabout, who was just getting out from under the Round Table.

"Well, the crystal must be there somewhere – but I'm blowed if I can find it! *AAAAARGH!*" he added, upon spotting the lions and tigers circling.

Demelza and Morag were picking themselves up and cackling as the big cats got closer and closer and prepared to pounce. But then the beasts paused, and began to back off a little.

"What's going on?" demanded Morag.

"And what's that funny noise?" asked Demelza.

There was indeed a very strange sound – like a very high, tuneless note on violin that sets your teeth on edge. Everyone's eyes turned to Sir Gadabout. He had dived back under the Round Table, and it was he who was quivering and emitting a fearful sound which hurt the sensitive ears of the animals.

"We could *all* make that noise!" said King Arthur.

"It's all right for you lot," complained Sidney Smith, pressing his paws over his own ears.

Nevertheless, they all began to imitate Sir Gadabout and make for the door. Sure enough, the lions and tigers howled and backed off, allowing everyone to escape.

"*Bah!*" said Demelza disgustedly. "I knew I wouldn't be queen for long. It's not fair – I was really enjoying it!"

"All is not lost, sister!" said Morag. With a wave of her hands and a few magic words, dozens of earplugs appeared out of nowhere and floated in the air. With another wave of her hands, they all shot into the ears of the animals.

"Now – FETCH!" She yelled, pointing towards the fleeing enemy.

Guinevere, who had been out of Camelot when it had been taken over and had managed to slip back inside to try and help, couldn't believe what she was seeing. King Arthur, Sir Gadabout, Herbert and Sidney Smith, were all running along and humming like broken violins!

"This is no time for a sing-song!" she exclaimed. "You're all out of tune anyway."

"We are scaring away some wild animals, Your Majesty," Sir Gadabout told her. "And it was my idea . . . well, sort of."

"Scaring them away?" replied Guinevere. "I wouldn't be so sure." She pointed to the lions and tigers swarming through the door of the Great Hall behind them.

Sir Gadabout jumped so fast and high that he left his armour behind and it fell

with a clang in a heap on the ground. "YAAAAAARGH!"

"Help is on its way," she said. "But until it arrives, we must escape and hide." Guinevere whipped out a packet of tacks she had been using for her last building project, and scattered them in front of the advancing lions and tigers. When the animals tried to go further, they began to hop up and down crying, *"Ouch! Ooyah! Oww!"* (But in tiger and lion language, obviously.)

This gave everyone time to run. Guinevere led them through a door into one of Camelot's tallest towers, and along various corridors. They turned so many corners that Sir Gadabout began to feel dizzy and wanted to stop for a bit. Luckily, Herbert, who was carrying baby Simon Pittance in one arm, was able to drag his master along with the other. Guinevere knew Camelot like the back of her hand (hardly surprising considering she was in charge of building it) and took them up some steep, narrow steps which led to a big oak door. When they opened it there was such a loud creaking sound that they were worried for a moment it might have given them away. They paused and listened, but Guinevere had led them to such a remote part of the castle that the coast seemed to be clear. They closed the door behind them and bolted it.

"No lions and tigers can get through *that*!" said Herbert.

"I'm sure Morag and Demelza have got other tricks up their sleeves," grumbled Sidney Smith.

"But you are forgetting – I still have the Crystal of Complexion!" announced Sir Gadabout, who, after jumping clean out of his armour, was now wearing only his vest and his favourite Barnacle Bill long johns. He raised the crystal aloft. "All I need to do is—"

"NOOO!" everyone else cried, and dived on him like rugby players.

There was such a scramble that Guinevere ended up wearing Herbert's gorilla suit, baby Simon Pittance was wrapped in

Guinevere's cardigan, Sidney Smith had Sir Gadabout's long johns on, and Sir Gadabout was wearing Guinevere's – well, we'd better not go into that.

"*Yuk!*" miaowed Sidney Smith when he saw what he had on. "Don't you ever wash these?"

"Of course I do!" Sir Gadabout replied. "Every Easter – even if they don't look dirty!"

Sidney Smith held his nose and wriggled out of them as fast as he could.

The room was full of carpentry tools and bits of wood of all shapes and sizes which Guinevere saved in case they came in handy for the next project. There was a large window which looked down into the courtyard of Camelot castle, and Sidney Smith crept up to it to see what was going on below.

"Bah! There's every type of wild animal under the sun down there looking for us. We're history!"

"We could clamber down the walls like those SAS people do!" Sir Gadabout suggested.

"They use ropes, you dope!" said Sidney Smith.

"Oh, do they? Well . . . we could *pretend* we've got ropes. The animals would never know!"

"But gravity would, mouse-brain." There came what sounded like a mouse-like squeak of indignation from a far corner of the room.

"The only way to escape from those beasts is if we could fly," sighed Herbert.

"That's it!" cried Guinevere, looking at all the wood and equipment surrounding them.

"By jove she's got it!" said Sir Gadabout, clambering onto the window ledge. "We can pretend we can fly!"

Herbert quickly pulled him back before he could come to any harm. "I think Her Majesty means we could build a plane, sire."

Guinevere quickly got to work with her tools, giving everyone little jobs to do in order to speed things up. "I have built a plane

before," Guinevere told them has they sawed and hammered. "But that one had twin-turbo afterburners and stealth technology. This one will have to glide, so it must be *exactly* the right shape and size." (For this reason, Sir Gadabout was only allowed to hammer the odd nail in, under strict supervision. Even then he managed to hammer Herbert's thumb and nail Sidney Smith's tail to a plank – luckily it was just the hairy part so it didn't hurt. Herbert seemed strangely disappointed about this . . .)

Such was Guinevere's genius that within a few minutes, they had completed a sleek glider: small enough to fit through the window, yet just large enough to carry them all.

"We'll fly over the walls of Camelot in the direction of Merlin's cottage," said the queen.

"As long as we don't get shot down by Dr McPherson," said Herbert. "He's got a tank!"

"Everyone had better be on the lookout, then," she replied with a slight smile – as if she knew something they didn't . . .

They lifted the plane on to the very edge of the windowsill and all clambered aboard, holding on as tightly as they could. Herbert was at the back. He gave them a big push-off – and away they flew!

7

Tanks for the Help

When Sir Gadabout looked down and saw just how far up in the air they were – and what kinds of wild animals were circling below, he let out a scream like one of those lady opera singers when they do a big finish and you can see their tonsils going up and down. Worse still, he began to tremble so violently that some of the nails in the plane started to work loose.

Herbert, who was still holding baby Simon Pittance in one arm, tried to hold Sir Gadabout with the other to stop him shaking. He held on so tightly that Sir Gadabout's shaking sent the baby to sleep.

Sidney Smith sniggered and shouted at the animals below as they flew over them. *"See yah – wouldn't wanna be yah!"*

Then Sir Gadabout, who had calmed down a little, whipped out the Crystal of Correction. "Let's bomb them!" he yelled.

"NO SIRE!" Herbert warned. He made a grab for the crystal – but not only did he not prevent Sir Gadabout from dropping it – he also dropped baby Simon Pittance!

"Universo – change it black!" shouted Sir Gadabout as he dropped his "bomb".

"You shouldn't have said that . . ." groaned Sidney Smith.

The spinning crystal began to send out blue flashes of light in all directions. One beam hit part of the wall of the tower they

had just left, and it turned into the original rocks which it had been made from (only blacker) and tumbled down. The animals below ran for their lives as the massive rocks came cascading towards them. Morag and Demelza had run out to see what was happening, and another beam struck them and turned their clothes back into the shaggy white sheep's wool they were made from – complete with the sheep!

"Eek!" they screeched, holding the struggling sheep tightly against them to cover their embarrassment.

In the meantime, Guinevere had skilfully guided the plane so that it swooped down and allowed Sir Gadabout to catch the falling baby Simon Pittance before he hit the ground.

Sir Gadabout pulled a funny face at the baby. *"Cootchy-cootchy coo!"* he warbled.

"In case it has escaped your attention," Sidney Smith pointed out, "we are all about to plummet to the ground and be eaten by lions and tigers."

"Not in this fine flying machine!" said Sir Gadabout.

Just then yet another blue beam snaked out of the falling crystal and hit their glider, turning it back into the tree its wood had come from.

"Aaaaargh!" cried Sir Gadabout. "On the other hand, you might be right!"

They all clung on grimly to the branches and twigs for dear life. The tree clipped the head of a charging rhinoceros, knocking him out before he could catch them, then came to a rather fortuitous soft landing in

the sand of the Camelot Crèche sandpit.

"That was lucky," Sir Gadabout remarked, plucking some leaves from his mouth.

"*That's* not!" said Sidney Smith. He was pointing his paw towards the animals – every type of savage beast you could think of was coming towards them with Morag and Demelza (who had thankfully cast a spell to give them more clothes) at their head.

"That's it!" wailed Sir Gadabout to baby Simon Pittance in his arms. "We're doomed! We've had it! We're all going to be animal

food!" He began to cry very loudly. Baby
Simon Pittance tried to cheer him up by
grinning and making burbling noises, but it
was no good – Sir Gadabout kept on
blubbing.

But then, just when the animals were so
close that their vicious snarls could be heard,
their gleaming teeth clearly seen, and Morag
and Demelza's evil laughter could be heard,
there came another sound. It was a rumbling
noise. It grew louder and louder, until,
through a hole in Camelot's mighty walls
made by the Crystal of Correction, came –
Dr McPherson in his tank!

"Look out – he's going to fire!" shrieked
Morag.

"Ha!" sneered Demelza. We'll see about
that!"

She whipped her magic wand out and chanted:

> *"Don't forget*
> *You've me to thank*
> *When my spell*
> *Bungs up his TANK!"*

Dr McPherson pressed a button.
  "FIRE!"

Nothing happened.
  "Tee-hee!" cackled Morag. "Well done, sister! Now we've got 'em. Forward, animals – dinner's on me!"
  "We're finished!" sobbed Sir Gadabout. "Ruined! Had it!"
  "Googly-goo!" grinned baby Simon

Pittance, but it was no good. Sir Gadabout wept so much that the poor little baby's head was soon wet through and he was coughing and spluttering.

Then there came another rumbling sound. They all thought it must be Dr McPherson turning round in his tank and going home. But he was still there, with his bunged up barrel pointing at Morag and Demelza. But the rumbling was definitely coming from his direction . . .

Then Dr McPherson's tank began to rattle. And then it began to shake. And the rumbling grew louder.

Morag looked at Demelza. "You stupid idiot!"

"What do you mean? I stopped him firing, didn't I?"

The tank began to throb. It began to judder.

A look of panic came over Dr McPherson's face. He had loaded it with double the amount of melons – and there was plenty more ammunition stored inside.

"You shouldn't have bunged up his barrel!" yowled Morag as the rumbling began to sound like thunder. "SHE'S GOING TO BLOW!"

"Everyone get down!" Guinevere warned her lot wisely.

"*WHAAAAAH!*" cried Dr McPherson. He struggled to climb out of the turret – but he was too late.

The rumbling grew deafening and the rattling became violent.

BOOOOM!

The poor guard-turtle was sent hurtling

skyward and was soon a tiny vanishing speck (he was eventually rescued by a passing space shuttle).

Morag and Demelza were knocked off their feet and so covered in melony goo that they couldn't move.

What they don't often tell you in wildlife programmes is that *all* savage wild animals are severely allergic to melons. They were covered in the stuff, and stampeded off in a mad panic through the gap in the wall, not stopping till they reached Bognor Regis (where as luck would have it the National Melon Disaster Animal Sanctuary is based).

Because they had thrown themselves to the ground, Guinevere and her crew had not been too badly affected. Herbert was able to jump to his feet and tie up Morag and Demelza, and Merlin was summoned to sort them out.

At the banquet afterwards to celebrate Camelot's lucky escape, Herbert told some of his squire mates, "You should have seen me in that gorilla suit! I looked like mighty

King Kong himself! I could have frightened all the animals off myself there and then — but I don't like cruelty to animals so I went easy on them."

"Those tigers are only really pussy cats like me but a bit bigger," Sidney Smith was telling Tibbles, the Camelot cook's cat, as they shared a saucer of melon juice. (Sidney had grown to quite like it.) "I think I could have taken at least a couple of them — they're not as nippy on their feet as me. But I

thought I'd better let someone else take the credit – if you act the hero too often people might think you're getting big-headed."

"And then the clever turtle frightened away the big, bad, naughty animals," said Sir Gadabout, feeding Simon Pittance a spoonful of mushed-up banana (he wasn't still a baby – but the spell does take a while to wear off *completely*). "And everyone lived happily ever after!"

"*Googly-gurgle-goo!*" said Simon Pittance. Which is baby talk for: although Guinevere and her team of builders soon made Camelot as good as ever, everyone knew that Sir Gadabout was *still* the Worst Knight in the World!